MW00962946

Too Much MacTiggle

Written by

Antionette Melendez

Illustrated by Ariane Elsammak

Balmore House
PUBLISHING

This book is dedicated to my son, Francisco, whose much-needed computer skills have allowed me to go from writing on paper to writing on the computer, and to my best friend, Melito, for reading rough draft after rough draft.

Balmore House Publishing
http://toomuchmactiggle.com

Too Much MacTiggle is distributed by DartFrog Books, which selects and represents the best in self-published literature.
DartFrog Books, PO Box 867, Manchester, VT 05254

Publisher's Cataloging-In-Publication Data
(Prepared by The Donohue Group, Inc.)

Names: Melendez, Antionette. | Elsammak, Ariane, illustrator.
Title: Too Much MacTiggle / written by Antionette Melendez ; illustrated by Ariane Elsammak.
Description: [Patterson, California] : Balmore House Publishing, [2017] | Manchester, VT : DartFrog Books | Interest age level: 004-008. | Summary: "He was too too much trouble. He made too much noise. Where in the world could this puppy find a home?"–Provided by publisher.
Identifiers: LCCN 2015917520 | ISBN 978-0-9969525-1-4 (paperback)
Subjects: LCSH: Scottish terrier—Juvenile fiction. | Puppies–Behavior–Juvenile fiction. | Dog adoption—Juvenile fiction. | CYAC: Scottish terrier–Fiction. | Dogs–Behavior–Fiction. | Dog adoption–Fiction.
Classification: LCC PZ7.1.M45 To 2017 | DDC [E]–dc23

Printed in the United States of America

Contents

Chapter 1

Trouble!

The little black Scottish terrier pup howled.

Awooooo! Awooooo! Awooooo!

His water bowl was empty and he was thirsty.

"Hey! How about some service around here, Mr. Teeply," the puppy called. "This is your pet shop, isn't it?"

The puppy's loud howling upset the other pet shop animals.

The monkeys chattered.

Oo-oo-ooo! Oo-oo-ooo!

The parakeets chirped.

Tweet! Tweet! Tweet!

Every other dog barked.

Woof! Woof! Woof!

But the little puppy's *Awoooooos* topped them all until he heard the loud stomps of footsteps coming close.

"Uh-oh," the pup whispered. "That could be Mr. Teeply."

And it was.

"Hey, you, little fellow!" Mr. Teeply shouted. "Stop making all this noise! Stop causing all this trouble!"

The puppy's pen sat in the middle of the shop so Mr. Teeply could keep his eye on the puppy. Spilled water was everywhere.

"My goodness! You've been a very busy puppy, haven't you?"

Mr. Teeply studied the puppy. He saw that his left ear drooped. His nose was too big. All four legs were too short and stubby.

"You're too much trouble and you're too noisy, too," Mr. Teeply declared.

He mopped up the water, then swept the floor. "No wonder no one will buy you."

The best he could do was to give the pup a name. "I'm calling you TOO TOO MUCH," Mr. Teeply told the puppy. "Because that's what you are! Too too much of everything!"

He smoothed the puppy's fur. "Now please be good so I can have a nice day."

Once Mr. Teeply left, the puppy hung his head. "I want to leave, too," he sighed, "with a new owner like all the other dogs, but no one wants me."

He wondered about his new name, Too Too Much. “Maybe I *am* too too much?”

He pulled on his droopy left ear. He scrunched his too-big nose and he tried to shake out each of his too-short and stubby legs.

That’s when the shiny silver latch on his cage caught his eye. “Hmmm,” he said, panting.

Before too long, his too-big nose made escaping too-too easy.

He broke free from his cage.

"Doggies, get ready to play!" he called.

The puppy tiptoed down each of the pet shop's aisles. "It's play time!" he whispered.

There, on all sides, were dogs of every shape and size. Big dogs. Short dogs. Furry dogs. Mutts.

And Mr. Teeply was nowhere to be seen!

Too Too Much used his too-big nose to unlatch each and every cage.

Soon, dogs were everywhere! They yapped and barked and *WOOF*ed, no matter how loudly the pup tried to shush them.

They pooped!
They peed!
They tore open bags of dog food!

The monkeys *Oo-oo-oo*-ed.
The parakeets *TWEET-TWEET*ed.

Then Too Too Much heard stomps and running. "Who let these doggies out?!"

The pup hung his head. "Me and my big nose! I'm in trouble again!"

Mr. Teeply let him know he sure was. "No wonder someone placed you on my doorstep three months ago!"

Mr. Teeply carried the pup to his pen, and this time he padlocked Too Too Much's cage.

"There's no way your too-big nose can unlatch THIS!" Mr. Teeply said. There were no head pats this time. No "Be good's." "You're too too much for me to keep, little fellow. So since I can't sell you, I'm giving you away."

Too Too Much listened as Mr. Teeply phoned in his newspaper ad. "I want it to read 'Free Puppy Available NOW!!!' with three exclamation points."

Right then and there, Too Too Much laid down and tucked his tail between his legs.

"I sure hope someone wants a free puppy!" he whispered.

Chapter 2

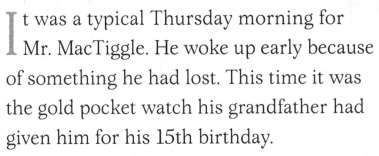

Three Strikes and You're Out!

It was a typical Thursday morning for Mr. MacTiggle. He woke up early because of something he had lost. This time it was the gold pocket watch his grandfather had given him for his 15th birthday.

Mr. MacTiggle searched everywhere, but all he found was a huge tear in his favorite blue chair. The tear was so big, he could almost fall inside it.

"I need you, Mrs. MacTiggle!" he called from the living room. But Mrs. MacTiggle didn't answer.

Had he lost her too?

But then a very pleasing smell caused his nose to wiggle. He ran to the kitchen.

Mrs. MacTiggle stood guard by the oven. She wore her favorite rainbow apron. "Guess who baked your favorite crunchy peanut butter snickerdoodle cookies, Mr. MacTiggle?"

Mr. MacTiggle smacked his lips. Those snickerdoodles were crunchy on the outside and warm and gooey on the inside.

"*Mmmm...mmmm...mmmmm,*" he said. He remembered the sweet taste. Then he scratched his head. "Now what was it I came here to tell you?"

Mr. MacTiggle sat down to think on a wooden chair, but the chair began to wobble.

"Don't tell me you forgot to fix that chair!" Mrs. MacTiggle cried. And now *she* was worried. Mr. MacTiggle had become VERY forgetful.

Once the cookies cooled, Mrs. MacTiggle made two cups of cocoa with mini rainbow marshmallows. They found two kitchen table chairs that *didn't* wobble. It was time to snack and read the morning paper. "Well, look here, dear!" Mrs. MacTiggle said. "Look at this ad for a free puppy!"

Mr. MacTiggle wiped peanut butter from his mouth. "I saw that earlier, but forgot to mention it."

"You know, I've wanted a puppy since I was a child, but we couldn't afford one," she shared.

Mr. MacTiggle smiled. "Well, here's our chance. This puppy is free!"

Mrs. MacTiggle quickly scribbled down the address of Mr. Teeply's Pet Shop on a recipe card. "Oh, I do hope no one else has seen this ad!"

Before anyone could say "crunchy peanut butter snickerdoodle cookie," Mr. MacTiggle was driving his little red car down the town's Main Street.

"Oh, jings!" Mr. MacTiggle cried. "I forgot that recipe card with the pet shop address!"

But just as he was turning back, he spotted Mr. Teeply's Pet Shop on the corner. He saw the sign for a free puppy hanging in the window.

"Fingers crossed," said Mr. MacTiggle as he rang the bell. "I hope I'm not too late."

The two *BRRRINNGGs* were the first of the day. Too Too Much tilted his head to the side and wagged his tail. "Could that be someone who wants a new puppy?"

He stood up to look on his too-short and stubby front legs.

Too Too Much heard a pleasant voice say, "I am Mr. MacTiggle. My wife and I are interested in your free puppy."

"That's *me!*" Too Too Much whispered, running around his pen. "That's *me!*"

But then he stopped. "What if he doesn't like my left droopy ear? Or my too-big nose? Or these too-short and stubby legs?"

But Mr. MacTiggle spoke very nice words that eased Too Too Much's mind. "By golly! You're a Scottish terrier puppy!" said Mr. MacTiggle. "Mrs. MacTiggle and I are Scottish, too!"

Too Too Much studied the man who owned the voice. The man wore a friendly smile and a blue sweater with twinkly gold buttons. His hair was the color of mixed salt and pepper.

Too Too Much stretched his too-short and stubby front paws through the cage. He wagged his tail and barked as fast as he could.

Ruff! Ruff! Ruff! "Today's the day I could be leaving!" he told himself.

Mr. MacTiggle patted Too Too Much's head. "Mr. Teeply says you're way too noisy...."

He tickled Too Too Much's right ear. "...and you cause too much trouble. So you'll be coming home with me..."

Too Too Much began wagging his tail again. "...but on a trial basis."

The wagging stopped. He blinked his eyes fast. *Trial basis?* He looked at Mr. Teeply. Mr. Teeply rubbed both of Too Too Much's ears.

"If you cause trouble three times, puppy, you'll be back here before you know it."

Mr. MacTiggle kneeled and looked Too Too Much in the eye. "Like they say in baseball, pup, three strikes and you're out!"

Too Too Much barked. *Ruff! Ruff! Ruff!*

"I can do this!" he whispered. "Someone wants me!"

ACTIGGLE

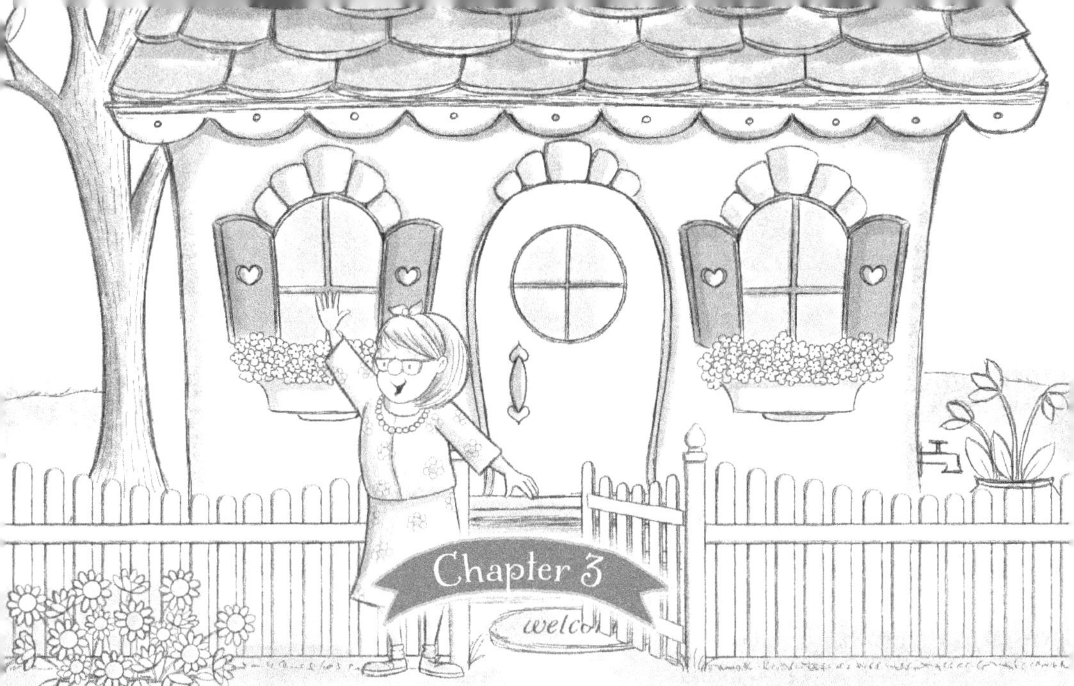

Chapter 3

Trouble for the MacTiggles

Too Too Much loved the ride home. He stuck his furry little head out the car window. The wind blew his ears back, tickling both.

He loved the MacTiggles' beautiful blue house with its white picket fence. "My new home!" Too Too Much whispered.

He loved how Mrs. MacTiggle hurried to the car and picked him up. "My goodness! You're absolutely adorable and Scottish, just like us!" she said.

Too Too Much's ears suddenly pointed up. He squirmed in her arms and licked her cheeks. *Slurp. Slurp. Slurp.*

"Does he have a name, dear?" Mrs. MacTiggle asked.

"Mr. Teeply named him Too Too Much. He said he was too much trouble and way too noisy," said Mr. MacTiggle.

"What a silly name for such a cute puppy," said Mrs. MacTiggle.

"Well, Mr. Teeply seemed to know what he was talking about. I agreed to bring him home, but on a trial basis."

"Whatever does that mean?"

Too Too Much looked from Mr. MacTiggle to Mrs. MacTiggle. He wagged his tail as fast as he could. He scrunched his too-big nose against Mrs. MacTiggle's cheek.

"The third time he causes trouble, dear, it's back to the pet shop. Right, puppy?" Mr. MacTiggle asked. He patted Too Too Much's head. "Now, off to find those sunglasses I lost!"

Mrs. MacTiggle kissed Too Too Much's droopy left ear. "I'm absolutely certain you'll be no trouble at all," she said. "Let's think about renaming you once you're ours for sure."

Ruff! Ruff! Ruff! Mrs. MacTiggle's words were music to both of Too Too Much's ears.

"Now let's get you some water in the kitchen. I bet you're thirsty."

The kitchen still smelled of those delicious, crunchy peanut butter snickerdoodles. Too Too Much's too-big nose twitched overtime. *Sniff. Sniff. Sniff.* He wiggled and squirmed in Mrs. MacTiggle's arms.

Soon, though, he sat on the floor before a small bowl of water. *Slurp. Slurp. Slurp.*

He put his left paw in the bowl and was happily drinking when Mrs. MacTiggle announced that it was time to water her prized backyard daisies. She'd been growing them all summer for the County Fair.

She left through the opened back door. "I bet they'll win first place again," she called.

Suddenly, Too Too Much looked up. "What was that?!" he whispered. He'd seen something big, brown and furry pop out of a hole in the ground. "And what's it doing in *my* backyard?"

Too Too Much needed to know. He darted for the open door, toppling his water bowl. Water spilled everywhere!

In a second, dirty little paw prints covered the MacTiggles' kitchen floor.

In three seconds, Too Too Much was *dig-dig-digging* inside Mrs. MacTiggle's flowerbed.

Daisies flew in every direction!

"Oh, my goodness!" cried Mrs. MacTiggle.

Too Too Much stopped digging and looked over. He trotted to the back door, shaking off as much dirt as he could.

Now Mr. MacTiggle stood beside his wife.

"No paws in my garden, puppy!" Mrs. MacTiggle warned Too Too Much.

"Maybe Mr. Teeply was right," Mr. MacTiggle said. His face wore a frown. "You might be too much trouble for Mrs. MacTiggle and me."

Too Too Much looked back at the empty flowerbed and hung his head.

"That's one," Mr. MacTiggle told him. He held up one finger. "One chance gone. Now stay put in this kitchen while Mrs. MacTiggle cleans up and I look for my sunglasses."

Too Too Much did his best. He *tried* to stay put. He let his eyes follow Mr. MacTiggle all around the kitchen and into the living room.

But suddenly his too-big nose began twitching again.

Sniff. Sniff. Sniff.

Someone had dropped one of those crunchy peanut butter snickerdoodle cookies. It was under the stove!

Too Too Much pushed his too-big nose this way and that as he broke the cookie into bits. He'd eaten just about every crumb when two round and dark circles caught his eye.

Ruff! Ruff! Ruff!

Ruff! Ruff! Ruff!

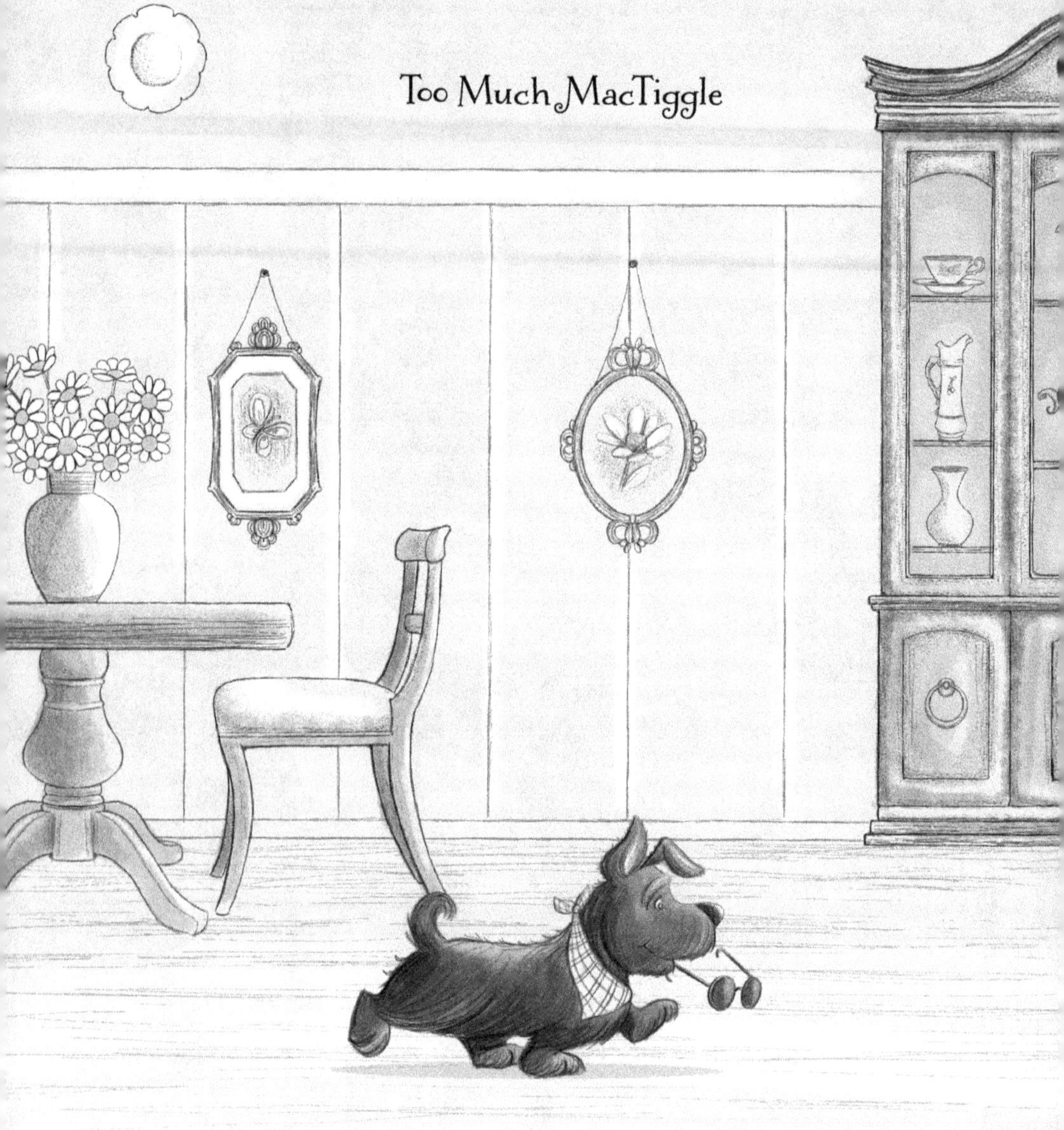

"Well, what do you know," Mr. MacTiggle said. "You found my lost sunglasses!"

Mr. MacTiggle scratched Too Too Much behind his furry little ears. "Thank you!" he said.

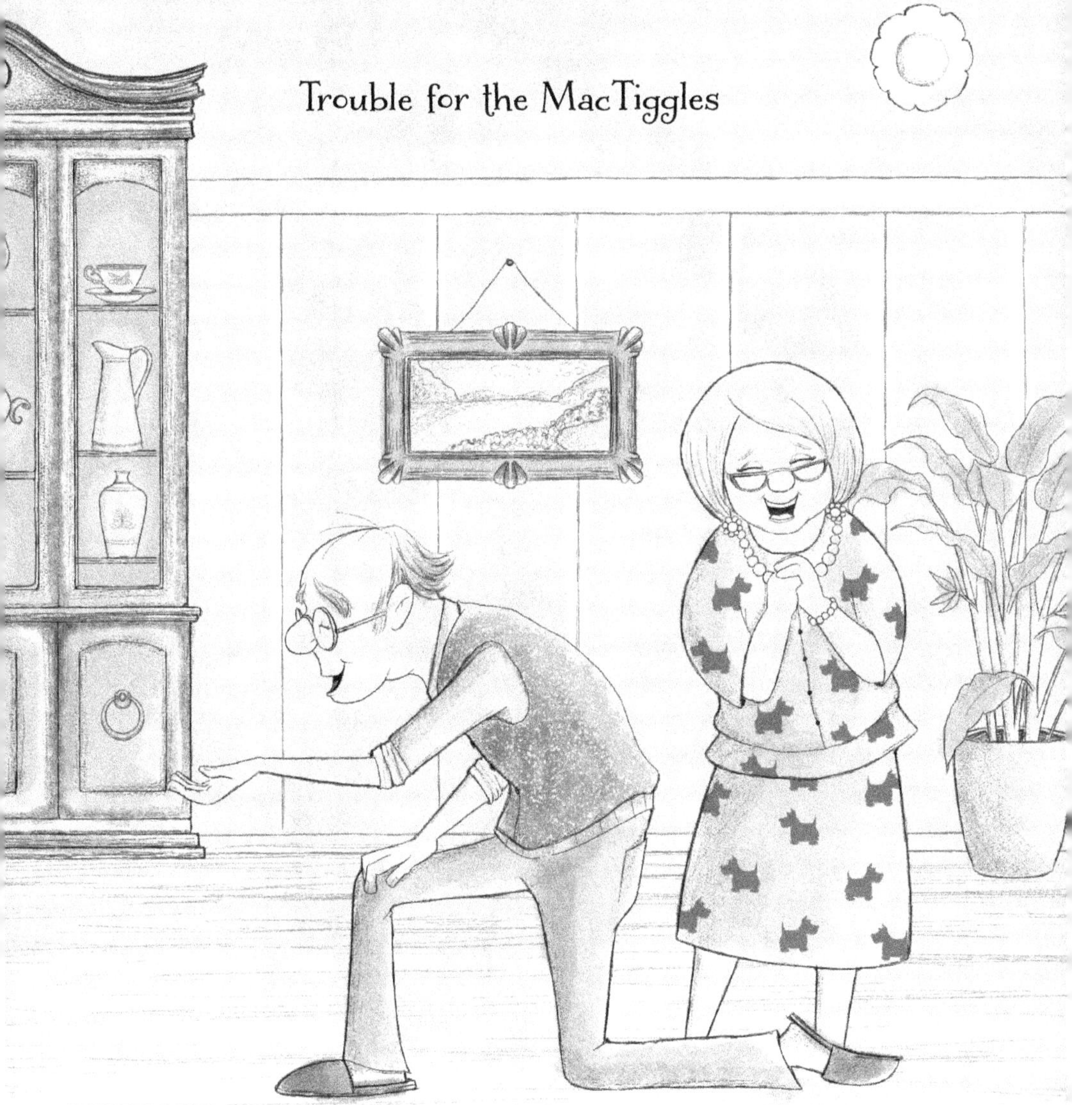

Too Too Much wagged his tail as fast as he could. He'd performed a good deed!

Mr. MacTiggle smiled. "No need to worry yet, little fellow. You still have two chances left."

Chapter 4

Saving the Day Again!

Too Too Much awoke the next morning to feel his too-big nose twitching. *Sniff! Sniff! UGH!*

What could smell so awful? he wondered. He followed his nose 'til he reached the kitchen.

"OH, NO!" he gasped.

Small gray clouds billowed from the oven. "SMOKE!" he gulped. "And SMOKE spells TROUBLE!"

Ruff! Ruff! Ruff! He ran around in circles. *Ruff! Ruff! Ruff!* He barked as loud as he could.

The MacTiggles rushed into the kitchen. "My cookies!" Mrs. MacTiggle cried. "Hurry, Mr. MacTiggle! My cookies are burning!"

The puppy watched as Mr. MacTiggle turned off the oven and carefully removed the pans of burnt cookies.

"Lucky for us we had our puppy!" Mrs. MacTiggle said. She rubbed Too Too Much's furry little head. "What you are is too, too smart!"

The puppy spent the rest of the morning chewing on his rubber bone. "Maybe Too Too Smart could be my new name?" he thought.

He was feeling proud. Warning the MacTiggles was his *second* good deed. "Two good deeds are better than two chances left!" he told himself.

Too Too Much counted the hall clock's twelve *Cuckoos*, then he raced to the kitchen for lunch.

But just as his nose had twitched to warn of trouble that morning, Too Too Much's right ear stood up straight. He tilted his head to the side. Strange sounds stopped him. *Slosh! Slosh! Slosh!*

Too Too Much tip-toed toward the sounds on quiet paws.

There, in the middle of a lit room, stood a wooden table. On top of the table sat a fish bowl. Inside the bowl swam two bright orange goldfish. They were playing tag.

Too Too Much laid his head on the floor and splayed out his front paws.

"I want to play, too!"

He stood up on his too-short and stubby front legs to play. But when his furry little paws landed on the table, the bowl wobbled and teetered. Soon, water spilled over the bowl's rim, onto the floor and in Too Too Much's face.

"By golly, I knew it!" Mr. MacTiggle cried, slipping in a puddle. He'd followed the puppy into the room.

Once he righted himself, Mr. MacTiggle looked Too Too Much in the eye. "No paws on the table!" he ordered.

Then he wagged two fingers in Too Too Much's face. "That's the second time you've caused trouble, puppy. You have one chance left."

Too Too Much hung his head.

Still, he could hear Mr. MacTiggle mumbling as he ran out the door. "Mr. Teeply was right! This pup's too much trouble!"

But he also heard his stomach. *Grumble! Grumble! Rumble!* Those fish had made him forget about lunch.

To Too Too Much's surprise, Mr. and Mrs. MacTiggle weren't in the kitchen. He barked loudly.

Ruff! Ruff! Ruff!

Still no one came.

Suddenly, his too-big nose twitched non-stop. *Sniff! Sniff! Sniff!*

Too Too Much smiled. He recognized the smell.

A fresh batch of crunchy peanut butter snickerdoodle cookies sat on the kitchen table. One or two or maybe even six would make the perfect puppy lunch!

Too Too Much looked down at his too-short and stubby legs.

Next he looked up at the too-high table. And that's when he spied the garbage can.

Before too long, Too Too Much had used his too-big nose to push the garbage can right beside a kitchen chair. He happily hopped from the garbage can to the kitchen chair to the kitchen table.

He was swallowing the last of the cookies when Mr. and Mrs. MacTiggle walked in from the garden. They'd been outside planting a new bed of daisies.

"That's it!" Mr. MacTiggle declared. "This was your last chance! No paws on ANY table! You are too, too much trouble!"

Once again, Too Too Much hung his head. *Sniffle! Sniffle! Sniffle!*

Mrs. MacTiggle rubbed both of his furry ears. "What he is, dear, is busy and smart," she said.

"Look how he found a way to reach the cookies!"

Too Too Much licked her face. "We need to give this puppy one more chance," she said.

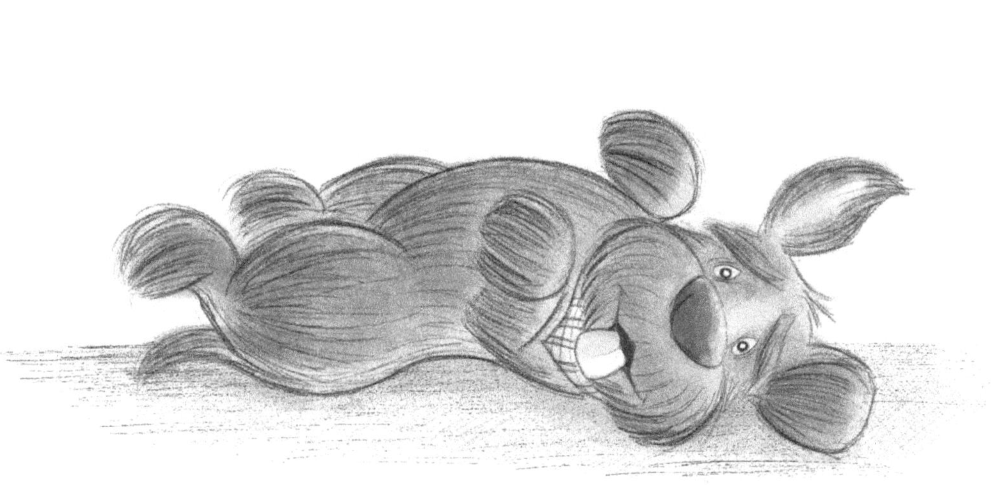

Chapter 5

Bad News

Too Too Much woke early Saturday morning. "Today I will not be too much trouble," he promised himself. "Instead," he declared, "I will look for my rubber bone."

No paws on the tables. No paws in the garden. Except, what were those shouts of "HELP!" coming from the living room? Was that Mr. MacTiggle? Was *he* in trouble this time?

Too Too Much raced to the living room. There he saw Mr. MacTiggle disappearing into his favorite blue chair!

Ruff! Ruff! Ruff! Ruff! Ruff! Ruff!

Mrs. MacTiggle came running in from the backyard, where she'd been watering her daisies.

"Oh, dear!" she cried. "We're losing Mr. MacTiggle to his favorite chair!"

She tugged with all her might on Mr. MacTiggle's legs. Soon he was standing on his own two feet.

"Phew and whew!" said Mr. MacTiggle. "I was still looking for my lost pocket watch!"

He pointed to the chair and the tear that needed fixing. "I knew I forgot to tell you something, dear."

"I'll fix it today," Mrs. MacTiggle promised. Then she picked up Too Too Much.

“Thank you!” she told him. She patted him twice on his furry head. “Once again, you saved the day!”

Too Too Much licked both her cheeks.

"That was my *third* good deed," he whispered. "I'll bet I'm here to stay."

He went looking for his bone after breakfast, but instead found Mr. MacTiggle's bedroom slipper.

Chewing was something Too Too Much did very well.

So he chewed and chewed until the slipper was soggy. Then he chewed its mate until it was soggy, too.

It was so much fun, he chewed four of Mrs. MacTiggle's slippers. But on his way out of the MacTiggles' bedroom, he slipped on a rug, slid into a hall table and OOPS! A vase of daisies fell to the floor. Water puddled everywhere.

Too Too much used his too-big nose to push the rug so it *almost* covered *most* of the spill. Then he spotted the roll of white paper in the bathroom. "Yes!" he whispered.

He pulled and pulled, unrolling the paper until it *almost* covered the puddles that were left.

He looked about. "Perfect!" he told himself. Off he trotted to find his missing rubber bone.

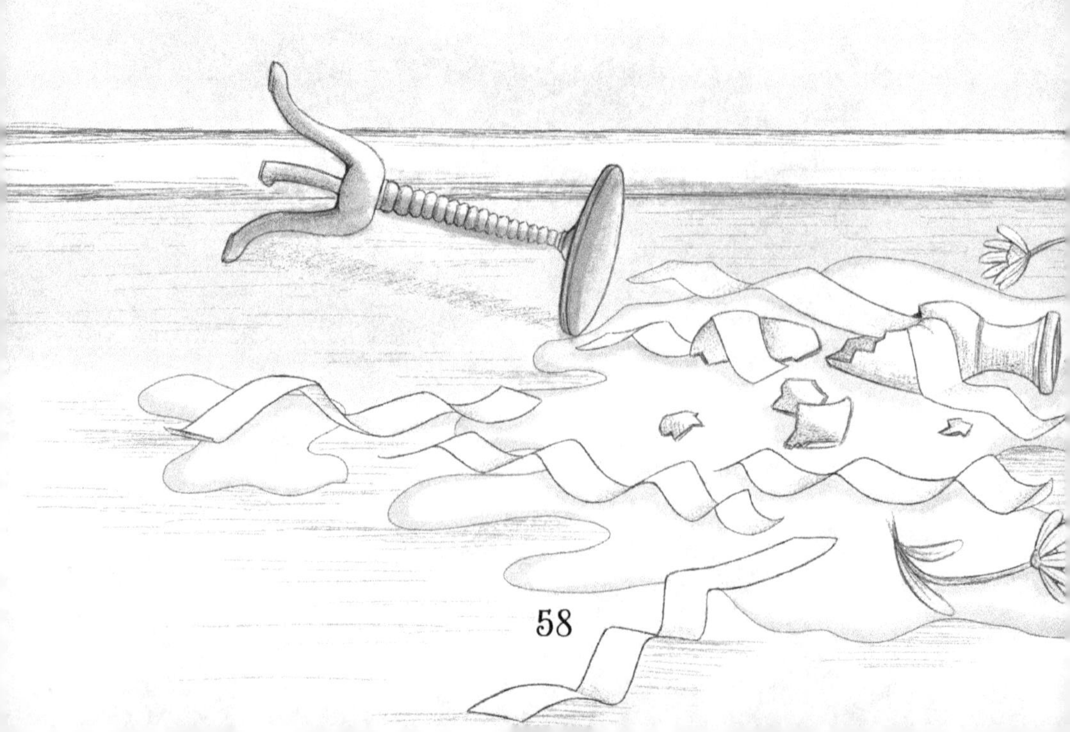

He looked here, there and everywhere, but couldn't find it.

"Maybe," he decided, "I left it *outside,* in the backyard?"

This time he'd look with only his eyes. Mrs. MacTiggle had said "No paws in the garden!"

But then there was that big, brown, furry thing again! It popped up from a hole beside Mrs. MacTiggle's flowerbed.

"You're not getting away *this* time!" Too Too Much shouted. He was off and running.

Ruff! Ruff! Ruff!

Suddenly that big, brown, furry thing dove into a hole in the middle of the flowerbed.

Too Too Much dug like there was no tomorrow! Before he knew it, he'd dug up Mrs. MacTiggle's flowerbed. AGAIN!

This time he didn't just hang his head. He laid down and tucked his tail between his too-short legs.

He covered both his ears, too. No way did he want to hear Mr. MacTiggle's words.

"You've made a mess in our bedroom, puppy!" Mr. MacTiggle shouted. He held up his chewed slippers to show Mrs. MacTiggle.

"Now you've torn up our garden again! This was your very last chance! It's back to the pet shop!"

Too Too Much looked up at the MacTiggles, then closed his eyes.

Chapter 6

A New Name!

Too Too Much buried his head inside his too-short and stubby front paws. He whined and whimpered softly. *Sniffle. Sniffle. Sniffle.*

"I thought the MacTiggles were the someones who would want me," he whispered. He sniffled once more. "But now tomorrow it's back to the pet shop."

After a while, he trotted inside for a drink of water. "Maybe I can still find my rubber bone," Too Too Much decided, "before the MacTiggles return me."

But a strange loud noise set his whole body jiggling. Once again he tilted his head to the side and wagged his tail. He pawed his way down the hall. It was Mrs. MacTiggle!

Or, rather, it was Mrs. MacTiggle's sewing machine. *Bzzzzlyd-Bzzle-Bzzle!* She was busy making a patch for the tear in Mr. MacTiggle's blue chair.

Mrs. MacTiggle stopped sewing and picked up Too Too Much. She stroked his droopy ear, then his too-big nose.

"You and I are *both* sorry you won't be staying, puppy. I think Mr. MacTiggle is sorry, too."

Too Too Much *ruff-ruff*ed. He rolled over in her arms. She rubbed his belly softly.

"By the way," she said. She put him on the floor. "You're not the only good finder. Here's your rubber bone. I found it beside the cuckoo clock."

Too Too Much pushed the bone this way and that with his too-big nose while Mrs. MacTiggle went back to sewing.

Bzzzzldy-Bzzle-Bzzle!

Ruff! Ruff!

Bzzzzldy-Bzzle-Bzzle!

Ruff! Ruff!

Before he knew it, he'd pushed his rubber bone beneath Mr. MacTiggle's yellow work bench. The bench wouldn't budge.

Suddenly, both his ears stood at attention. *Tick! Tock! Tick! Tock! Tick! Tock! Tick!*

His two puppy eyes spied something twinkling. Was it a shiny gold button from Mr. MacTiggle's sweater?

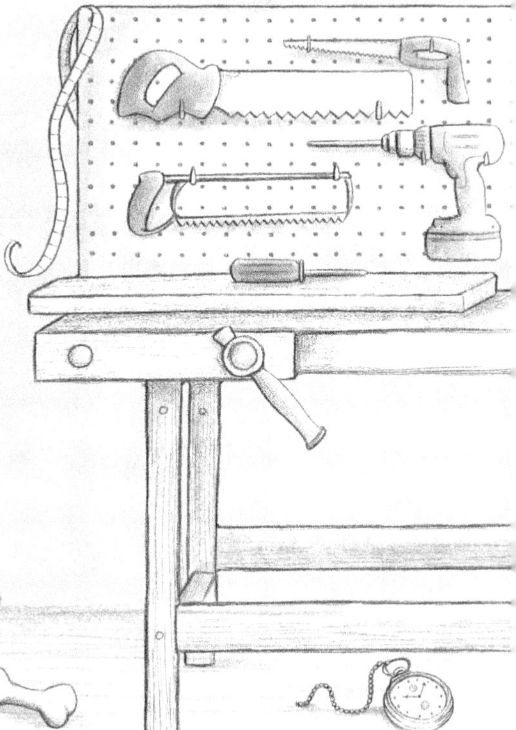

Ruff! Ruff! Ruff! Mrs. MacTiggle stopped sewing.

Ruff! Ruff! Ruff!

Too Too Much ran in circles.

"My goodness, puppy! What did you find this time?" she asked.

Mrs. MacTiggle pushed the bench aside.

"By golly!" shouted Mr. MacTiggle. He'd come huffing and puffing because of all the noise.

"That's my grandfather's pocket watch! I found it! I found it!"

Mrs. MacTiggle *harrumphed.* "Excuse me, dear, but that isn't quite so."

She picked up Too Too Much, held him high, and kissed his droopy ear.

"This little puppy is the World's Best Finder. We need to keep him!"

Too Too Much wiggled and squirmed in her arms while licking her cheek. *Slurp! Slurp! Slurp!*

Mr. MacTiggle shook his head. "Except, think of your garden, dear! Think of our slippers! Think of the mess and noise! He's too too much trouble!"

"What he is, dear, is too busy, smart and curious. What he is, dear, is too much PUPPY!"

Too Too Much *RUFF-RUFF-RUFF*ed and wagged his tail fast.

"Well," said Mr. MacTiggle. He smooched Too Too Much's nose. "I do seem to lose things..." He tickled Too Too Much's right ear. "and he *is* a good finder."

Mrs. MacTiggle smooched the pup's nose, too. "You're a keeper alright, and I have the perfect name for you."

The puppy became still. Both his ears straightened.

"What do you think of Too Much MacTiggle?"

"Too Much MacTiggle?" The puppy repeated the new name to himself. He blinked nonstop. Then he wagged his tail.

He pulled his droopy left ear close enough to study it. He scrunched and un-scrunched his too-big nose. He carefully examined his too-short and stubby legs.

"The MacTiggles think I'm just enough!" he whispered.

He gave his best puppy howl.

Awooooo! Awooooo! Awooooo!

Too Much MacTiggle had found his someones.

About the Author

Ms. Melendez (Tonie) was born in Baltimore, Maryland. Currently living in Patterson, California, the apricot capital of the world. Growing up, she always had her head in a book and continued to do so. She recalls her mom saying "lights out you have school tomorrow." She replied "ok mom." But when the coast was clear the lights would pop back on. She would reach under her bed and pull out a book. "Just a few lines before falling asleep" she would say. Her mom never knew.

She works for the Veterans Administration as a nurse and has received numerous nursing awards for her dedicated service to veterans.

Her son, Francisco, lives in Las Vegas. He's the joy of her life. She smiles when thinking about all the times they had spent together reading books when he was a child.

The inspiration for her children's book Too Much MacTiggle came from her little black Scottish terrier named Rhoj AKA Doodles. The nosiest dog ever! A combination of Scooby Doo and Inspector Clouseau all rolled up into one big fur ball. After reading this book, you'll know why she named the delicious cookies loved by the MacTiggles "Crunchy Peanut Butter Snickerdoodle Cookies."

About the Illustrator

Ariane Elsammak started drawing at a very young age and has been a freelance illustrator for the past 25 years. Her specialty is whimsical illustration and she most enjoys working on children's books as well as other projects for children's media. A mother of two grown children, she lives in New Jersey with her two dogs, Bogey and Toby. Visit her on the web at www.artbyari.com.

Acknowledgments

I would like to give special thanks to those who helped to make this book a reality. They offered essential support, reassurance, encouragement, and assistance in the proofreading, editing, illustration, and design of this book. I would like to thank Roger for pushing me to write this book. Many thanks to my son, Francisco, for putting up with me asking him question after question regarding how to use my new computer. I would like to thank my best friend, Melito, for always saying, "You can do this, Tonie!" Many thanks to Esther Hershenhorn for her editing skills and for brainstorming with me. Thanks to Ariane Elsammak, illustrator, for her creative attention to detail. Also, I give thanks to the staff at TLC Graphics, especially Monica Thomas who designed the layout and interior of this book. But most of all, I give thanks to my dog, Rhoj AKA Doodles, whose zany antics inspired me to write this book.